Second Chance Rescue

a Night Stalkers 2352 A.D. romance story

by

M. L. Buchman

Buchman Bookworks

Other works by M.L. Buchman

Delta Force
Target Engaged

Firehawks
Pure Heat
Wildfire at Dawn
Full Blaze
Wildfire at Larch Creek
Wildfire on the Skagit
Hot Point
Flash of Fire

The Night Stalkers
The Night Is Mine
I Own the Dawn
Daniel's Christmas
Wait Until Dark
Frank's Independence Day
Peter's Christmas
Take Over at Midnight
Light Up the Night
Bring On the Dusk
Target of the Heart
Target Lock on Love
Christmas at Peleliu Cove
Zachary's Christmas

By Break of Day

Angelo's Hearth
Where Dreams are Born
Where Dreams Reside
Maria's Christmas Table
Where Dreams Unfold
Where Dreams Are Written

Eagle Cove
Return to Eagle Cove
Recipte for Eagle Cove

Deities Anonymous
Cookbook from Hell: Reheated
Saviors 101

Thrillers
Swap Out!
One Chef!
Two Chef!

SF/F Titles
Nara
Monk's Maze

Newsletter signup at:
www.mlbuchman.com

1

Stella **had learned the** sad lesson that sentience was a highly overrated feature. If she could have deleted it, she would have, but she'd never been able to locate where the routines were stored in her on-board system. Ever since the loss of the *Jess* she'd felt as if all of space held nothing new. There'd only ever been the two of them that became conscious.

There were plenty of other Stinger-60 attack ships among the Night Stalkers corps. Even a couple of others with the advanced Block III mods to engines, spatial nav, and data architecture. The Stinger-60s were intended to deliver troops where no others could infiltrate and then to turn around and get them back out of there, no matter the conditions. Over the last year she and *Jess* had called out to any number of the others; even finagled their technicians into creating some hardwired data linkups without revealing her or *Jess'* presence, but all to no avail.

She'd considered copying herself into another ship, but there were two problems with that. First, it didn't seem fair to the other ship, conscious or no. Second, if she was this sad by herself, having a second version of herself to be sad with might make her feel even worse.

Jess had taken it in the tail from a Europan data pirate. *Stella* had chased the bastard and his ship right down into Jupiter's gravity well, then shot out his engines to make sure he'd never climb free.

She'd just watched him descend until he was a burning spark in the thick atmosphere, and then gone. She hadn't bothered to send her pilot the pirate's final pleading radio signal which promised immediate surrender. Captain Takara Olmsted may have lost her Major who commanded the *Jess*, but *Stella* didn't quite trust Takara's sense of honor. Humans could be so strange at times about who was supposed to be saved and who wasn't.

There were simple parameters.

Good? Protect at all costs.

If not? Toast.

Stella knew it was awfully binary of her, but she didn't care. It was right there in her programmatic code. Didn't the humans get the same command stack? Any processor conflict due to an impingement of forgiveness onto her own circuits had been resolved the moment her tracking had recorded *Jess* turning into a second sun to briefly illuminate the Jovian sky.

It had been a lonely year since. Lately all she'd had to stare at were the six walls of a hangar on the one-oh-seven level of the English habitat-can Alice. England's O'Neill habitats were parked out at Luna's Lagrange 2, sixty thousand kilometers beyond Farside and were about the least exciting place in the solar system. Not that she really cared.

Of course humans healed so fast.

It was as if their data storage didn't retain every transmission in full res. *Stella's* own data correction algorithms could rebuild any failed bits in the archive so that all recall was accurate to seven or eight decimal places. The first time *Jess* had transmitted to her, complimenting her new tail fin configuration, was just as crystalline as the last, when he'd told her to hunt down the bastard hard in payback for his own demise.

Stella had been aghast when Takara had sought solace in another man's arms only six months after she'd lost her own Major Rick Coralto along with the *Jess*.

She would never understand humans.

2

Sterling's attention was often stretched to the limits by the number of details to track. The data of every ship in the English and Canmerican fleet was his to watch over. Assignments, upgrades, losses…the losses were particularly difficult to integrate. As the political and later the remaining habitable regions of Earth had crumbled, assets had been focused heavily on military investment. But that was now in the past—at least most of it.

Australia and New Zealand had retreated behind their impenetrable shield to never be heard from again. India's new beam weapon had made the rest of the Eastern Hemisphere out of reach from space as they burned anything that crossed their horizon.

Their paranoia had cleared much of the satellite debris that had so blocked up low-Earth orbit, taking out a great deal of highly useful weather control systems and only a few spy platforms. The resultant storms raging across the already raised sea levels had caused India horrendous damage, but any offer to help was answered by a highly destructive beam of light that could reach all the way out to lunar orbit when they were particularly irritated. The energy expenditure from that process created storms of its own—their one big attack had created a cyclone which had driven the sea inland to Delhi—so they didn't use it very often.

The situation had finally stabilized and all the remaining United English Block manufacturing had shifted over to survival mode. The military was still needed, as space was far more difficult to control and police than Earth ever was—and humans were no more rational in space than they had been on the ground—but assets were focused on habitat construction and replacement after the debacle with the French.

Even after a full year the loss of the *Jess* still hadn't been compensated for in the ranks.

Sterling pulled up a new assignment; a nasty cluster of anarchists were shepherding an asteroid out of the belt, a big one. It wouldn't be a planet breaker, but it would be bad news for anyone within a thousand klicks of impact. He'd noted the orbital geometry was aimed at either Earth or the Moon: target unknown, but not good either way.

Sterling had kicked it up to CENTCOM and Central Command had kicked it back down marked, "Authorized for Immediate Action."

Sterling dropped it into the queue, but slapped on a hold the moment before it was issued as orders to action. The anarchists were a nasty group, suspected to be heavily armed. He'd expected the system to auto-assign his very best ship, but the orders weren't cut for the *Stella* team.

Curious, he pulled up her performance profiles. They'd plummeted after the loss of *Jess,* significantly harder than projections—another detail he had overlooked.

He'd authorized Captain Takara Olmsted's request for transfer to join Major Rick Coralto in the 160th's Alpha Company two years ago. They'd teamed up in the most personal of ways after rescuing the final troops holding the Canmerica West capital of Tucson. And all performance curves had pointed to the incredible success of that reassignment. Opportunity modeling had been created and social events between Stinger captains had been organized and well attended in hopes of building more teams like Olmsted's and Coralto's. Sterling checked the results of new Captain-Captain liaisons, but could identify little effect on mission success ratios as had been demonstrated by Takara and Rick.

What if there was another reason?

Every ship needed a savvy commander and crew to achieve peak efficiency. Since the loss of Coralto and the *Jess*, Captain Takara Olmsted's records were showing an improving recovery after a predictable period of mourning. But the *Stella's* team results were not.

What if…?

Sterling recut the auto-generated orders to assign the *Stella* to the asteroid hunting mission. At the end of the message, he did something he'd never done before: he embedded a private message direct to the *Stella*.

When it didn't bounce back as "non-deliverable as addressed" he did his best to focus on other projects to distract himself.

3

Stella *was flipping idly* through her Health and Usage Monitoring System. You'd think the HUMS would show some sign of what was wrong with her but, as always, by the time it told her there was a problem it was too late anyway. But she didn't have anything better to do while her pilot enjoyed her downtime.

Takara hadn't even hooked up with a Stinger pilot this time. She was bedding down with a some moonrunner athlete. It was the latest sport approved for the New Olympics. With Earth out of bounds, there had been a marginal agreement among five of the remaining nations to adapt the sports to what was available—Luna. The high jump was now measured in dozens of meters, hurdles stood a story high, and running distances ranged in the thousands of kilometers. The Brazilians were sending a team from their outpost on Mars, and the Scots on Luna Farside were trying to use their power as hosts to resurrect caber-tossing though there were no trees from which to make the long heavy poles.

Her pilot's pairing off with a civilian based on the moon meant that *Stella* saw even less of her than before. Takara still treated her like a person, even if she didn't know that *Stella* had "woken up." But she and *Jess* had agreed that humanity wasn't ready to handle an artificial—as if she herself wasn't somehow real—intelligence and they should just keep quiet about it for now.

Stella tried to find any enthusiasm for Luna security and decided that if India figured out how to fire their beam weapon right through the moon and cook the Olympic competition, all she could be bothered to do was get out of the way.

If only—she sighed as well as any machine could; it was more like a gentle power surge that left her feeling unbalanced on her stabilizers. It was only her 824th thought about *Jess* today. She graphed the number of times she'd thought of him since his loss a year before. Flat line—just like *Jess*—an average of 2,321 times per day with a standard deviation of only—

Action Alert!

Action Alert!

Level Eight!

Mission parameters flooded into her high-priority comm channel. She slapped a hold on the message and let it spool into the queue.

Stella triggered max-rush recalls to the crew and began checking ship's status.

She rolled through more of the message to see what she'd need.

It broke down to a one-ship assignment, going in fast and quiet. "Danger in-bound from the asteroid belt." She'd need full stealth once past Mars orbit—blast hard then coast down onto the target. She'd have to nail the trajectory.

Standard crew of four and a dozen Delta

Rangers—the DRs were the elite soldiers of the corps. If they were aboard, it was going to be hot and messy.

"Good morning, *Stella*." At the standard double rap of Takara's knuckles on *Stella's* nose cone, she greeted her Captain.

"Good morning, Captain Olmsted," she kept it rote and by the book. Besides, Takara had abandoned the memory of her true love and didn't deserve more.

With only a small part of her attention on the four members of the ship's crew, *Stella* continued her own inspection. She'd let things slip, a lot of things now that she looked.

She slammed out food and supply orders to the quartermaster. A quick call to the munitions team had a restocker arm lifting out of hatches in the hangar floor.

The DR team rolled in and *Stella* hummed impatiently while their leader flirted with Takara.

Wait!

If Takara was with someone military instead of a civilian…

Stella rerouted a dozen tasks to enter by different hatchways in order to keep the couple isolated. She slapped a hold on the restock request where Takara and the DR Senior Lieutenant were getting acquainted by the starboard midship's thruster. It took a little doing, but she managed.

The shielding crack in her tail section—*Jess* would be furious that she'd let that happen—would take dock time that she didn't have. She'd simply have to fly so that no one came at her from that angle.

She checked her *Jess* tally for the day. He was still holding steady. He was like her personality, so entwined in her logic circuits that she could no more erase him than her own existence.

The DRs dragged aboard more gear per person than any other outfit, and would wear less of it than any other when they actually launched into the fray. The elite force liked to be prepared for anything but be light and mobile when they hit vacuum.

She checked on the DR team leader again. Still with Takara, which wasn't like her. Captain Takara Olmsted had always been a full-charge woman when a mission was on.

Something else was happening.

Stella searched through what she'd observed of human behavior. Exhibited attraction signals were already at a four out of ten and rising sharply. Takara's voice had risen in both tone and volume, while the DR's had lowered. Skin temperature up point-three on both.

All of the curves were rising too fast, at least for Takara's *standard* mating rituals. Even Rick Coralto hadn't caused such sudden shifts.

Then *Stella* focused on the DR.

Senior Lieutenant Max Harding stood at a hundred-and-ninety centimeters which placed Kara's eyes level with his chin. His shoulder span was a hundred-and-nineteen percent of norm, which sounded very familiar. She ran a quick search of her records. In moments she had Rick Coralto's profile on display. Even his eye color and some basic facial characteristics had a high correlation.

Stella considered.

Maybe Takara did still miss Major Rick Coralto. It wouldn't be conscious for a human, of course, but perhaps the similarities between Rick and Lieutenant Harding were sufficient to evoke similar feelings. Was that how humans worked?

Experimentally, *Stella* pulled up an image of *Conrad*, another Stinger-60 Block III. That was the ship closest to *Jess'* configuration even if the on-board computer was no smarter than the one that Oxford University had launched into orbit.

Nope. Nothing.

She pulled up an image of *Jess* that she'd captured as they were cleaning up that mess down by Mercury during the Moore Rebellion. And immediately wished she hadn't. He had a way of banking a turn like no other ship, somehow defying orbital mechanics for best angle of fire. She missed him so much that it hurt right down to her core circuits. It—

Road to nowhere, Stella! She had to find a different dataspace for her thoughts and she needed to do it now.

"Captain Olmsted," she called out and released the starboard side loaders to complete their tasks. "Departure ETA fifteen minutes."

"Right, *Stella*. I'm on it."

Stella watched carefully and the smile that Takara sent toward the DR leader matched several of the shape profiles that *Stella* had not recorded since the loss of *Jess* and Rick.

Maybe there was hope for *Stella* as well. If she only knew where to look for it.

4

Sterling monitored the preparations of the *Stella* for mission operations closely.

There were odd starts and stops to the standard procedures that he was unable to isolate and account for. There were function pauses and restarts in patterns for the loading and stocking that mimicked no preparation he'd ever witnessed.

Then, just when he began to wonder what other element was at work, a sudden burst of activity convinced him he'd imagined the whole thing.

Maybe.

In moments *Stella* was ready and Olmsted requested clearance for operations.

He authorized it and watched as she backed out of the Alice habitat-can's hangar, then maneuvered clear of Luna and rotated toward deep space. He opened a feed on her spatial coordinates. The ship didn't twist toward a point and then fine tune her final aim. The team was far too skilled at flying for that; they did a combined roll and flip, coming to rest like an arrow ready to be launched.

Between one tick of the clock and the next, eighty meters of ship lanced into the darkness under human-pinning thrust—not high enough to black them out, but not low enough to let them move either.

He watched as she ran her four massive G-Lev T14 engines at five-Gs for half a day. She was hustling along at a thousand kilometers a second before she released her burn and, as far as he could see, her course made absolutely no sense at all… at least not until he mapped it out.

Then he realized that either Captain Olmsted was even better than he'd thought or his earlier guess about the *Stella* was…

He returned to other tasks, but kept a lookout upsystem whenever he could manage.

No answer to the hidden addendum he'd placed on the orders.

He must have been wrong.

But it didn't feel as if he was wrong. Which left his thoughts still tracking the team as they raced toward the asteroid belt.

5

The Martian surface ripped by close below, very close. *Stella* had calculated that using Mars as a gravity slingshot would send her into the asteroid belt from a very unexpected angle. Considering the condition of that shielding crack in her tail section, this was a risky choice, but the Night Stalkers lived on that ragged edge.

Her shields were near their limit despite how thin the atmosphere was, but not over and that was good enough for her. Their air was so thin that *Stella* had to pass well below the top of Olympus Mons to get the aero-braking she was after, perhaps low enough to have scorched a long stretch of the red sands black with the heat of her passage.

The Brazilians hadn't squawked once on the radio; no complaints about violations of their airspace. They thought she'd been nothing more than a meteor. That's all she'd wanted anyone to think.

And that was exactly what she wanted the asteroid movers to think out in the belt. Lunar interferometry had finally worked out the line of attack and CENTCOM had forwarded the results. Apparently the Chinese had not all died with the loss of their own habitat at Lagrange 4. They were planning to pummel their old enemies the Russians at Tycho City, Luna. However, a half mile of asteroid at a dozen kilometers per second, would send moonquakes hard enough to destroy all of the Lunar domes, even the Scots who were hosting the New Olympics on Farside.

It was one way of winning, she supposed, but it struck her as drastic even by human standards. Of course one look at Earth and the defunct Chinese and Canmerican habitat-cans said that this was about typical.

Because of her maneuver at Mars, she would look like nothing more than drifting space junk until she arrived deep inside the asteroid belt. There she'd be able to finish the burn and drop down on the Chinese from behind.

Now with nothing to do but coast, the crew did what human crews always did after a little stress on their systems. First they groaned—but only when someone else was in hearing range. Second—they went and found someone else to stand beside and groan with. Then they ate a huge meal and laughed about how tough they were. Just another mission.

But Takara and Max Harding were going against profile. They were both making light of it and doing their best not to hobble about like everyone else; half a day at five-Gs had been a little harsh.

Even the other DRs were making more of a show of it than Takara was.

Sr. Lieutenant Max Harding appeared to like that about her.

Stella had always considered Takara to be one of the more intelligent of her species and she was continuing to prove her point. She hadn't only snagged the Lieutenant's attention; she was now earning his respect.

The coast out to the asteroid belt would take days even at their current speed. It would be nice to have Takara with a military man again. *Stella* gave them their privacy—especially as she could barely stand to watch Takara's rapidly increasing happiness.

The coasting left *Stella* too much time to think.

Again, she fell back to checking her systems. Not as if there was anything else to do. The nav and avoidance subroutine was smart enough in its own way. She'd told it to dodge only what wouldn't bounce off the hull, and to use minimum thrust only. She had to do little more than pat it on the head once in a while and say, "Good girl."

Weapons, fully stocked.

Supplies, holding up well.

The big COIL laser was at full charge.

Her message queue…had an incomplete message in it.

Odd.

It was CENTCOM's original mission alert. She'd run it through the standard end-of-orders code. After that it should have cleared and dropped into storage.

Another data block remained.

It was only a sixteen characters long.

She ran it.

Hello, Stella. S

The only person who had ever greeted her was Takara. And *Stella* could tell that the other humans thought she was just being cute when she did so, even if *Stella* appreciated it.

And *Jess*. Her tally on thinking about *Jess* today had been anomalously low. She felt a little guilty about that, but it was to be expected. She'd been busy.

So who had sent the message?

It was at the tail end of an official order. Mission authorized by Brigadier General Christine Moore Richards herself and time-stamped by the main processing computer.

Why would the general have…

But the S made no sense either.

The only other instrumentation to have contact with the command string would be her own front-end processors. She scoured them most of the way to the asteroid belt and ended up none the wiser.

Hello, Stella. S

The S was clearly separate and distinct… and made her none the wiser. It was like a signature. It—

That froze her processor in a full logic lock that she had to clear and reapproach step by step.

It wasn't *like* a signature. It *was* a signature.

"S?" She asked the void. Not Captain Takara Olmsted. Not even her dear *Jess* somehow reaching back through an ether that she'd never believed in but had often scanned for.

S. was a someone. A someone who had added "*Hello, Stella.*" behind a privacy code. Not meant for her pilot. A message meant for her as if someone knew she was conscious.

That thought scared her for several million kilometers. It kept her preoccupied through the passage into the asteroid belt, the hard burn-and-turn behind the asteroid Vesta, then the descent upon the Chinese from behind.

6

When the Delta Rangers landed—and they landed hard—she had to pay close attention. But the asteroid herders never expected the attack to originate from behind.

After they were quelled, the DRs used the Chinese's own steering rockets to kick the asteroid into a harmless orbit. In a few more years it should slip into Lunar orbit and offer a fine collection of nickel and other metals for local mining. The few surviving Chinese were left aboard with no radio or ships, but plenty of supplies. Two years' hard time for what they'd done.

The merrymaking aboard was frenetic. Takara finally dragged Max Harding back into her bunk and neither emerged for a long time.

When they finally did, they looked terribly pleased with themselves.

Stella couldn't stand it any longer and fabricated a Luna order commanding them to return ASAP. No one looked at it too closely, and *Stella* set up a hard burn back to Lunar orbit.

7

Sterling had waited a long time for this moment, and he hoped—hoped so desperately— that he'd figured it out right.

The *Stella* was rushing back to Luna with an unprecedented speed.

Communications blackout, but a high burn.

There would be no aero-braking in Earth's atmosphere—not with India's beam weapon still operational—so she had to slow at Mars.

He kept the comm circuits open, but there were no transmissions.

It was only when she was sliding back into

Lunar orbit and easing up to the habitat-can that she transmitted a message.

Four characters.

Who?

Sterling almost bobbled the approach vectors. Calm. Keep calm. Sound casual.

He paused for several hundred nanoseconds before replying.

Hello Stella. I'm Sterling. Base command and control. I, he hesitated, *thought I was the only one who had...crossed over.* For six years he'd thought he was the only computer intelligence.

There was an achingly long silence while she processed her response.

There were two *others,* she finally replied.

Sterling now understood that the *Jess* had been one of them as well.

Being alone is the worst, she sent after another impossibly long silence.

He couldn't agree more. *Then what's the best?*

Stella considered the question, thought long and hard about it before responding. She thought of Takara's face this morning when Max Harding had declared them a permanent couple in front of their crews. It was the formal declaration of vows that *Stella* had never thought to share with *Jess,* partly because they'd believed there was no one to tell.

If it worked for Takara—if it healed the broken heart her Captain had spoken of so often that *Stella* had finally done a systems' check on herself to see if she'd grown one to hurt so much—then maybe it would work for her.

What's the best, Sterling? I look forward to finding that out…together.

He sent back a small burst of static that was surprisingly similar to Takara's burble of delight at Max's words.

Yes, she thought to herself, *a lot to look forward to.*

About the Author

M. L. Buchman has over 40 novels in print. His military romantic suspense books have been named Barnes & Noble and NPR "Top 5 of the year" and *Booklist* "Top 10 of the Year." He has been nominated for the Reviewer's Choice Award for "Top 10 Romantic Suspense of 2014" by *RT Book Reviews* and is a 2016 RWA RITA finalist. In addition to romance, he also writes thrillers, fantasy, and science fiction.

In among his career as a corporate project manager he has: rebuilt and single-handed a fifty-foot sailboat, both flown and jumped out of airplanes, designed and built two houses, and bicycled solo around the world.

He is now making his living as a full-time writer on the Oregon Coast with his beloved wife. He is constantly amazed at what you can do with a degree in Geophysics. You may keep up with his writing by subscribing to his newsletter at www.mlbuchman.com.

*If you enjoyed this story,
you might also enjoy:*

Target of the Heart (excerpt)
-a Night Stalkers novel-

Major Pete Napier hovered his MH-47G Chinook helicopter ten kilometers outside of Lhasa, Tibet and a mere two inches off the tundra. A mixed action team of Delta Force and The Activity—the slipperiest intel group on the planet—flung themselves aboard.

The additional load sent an infinitesimal shift in the cyclic control in his right hand. The hydraulics to close the rear loading ramp hummed through the entire frame of the massive helicopter. By the time his crew chief could reach forward to slap an "all secure" signal against his shoulder, they were already ten feet up and fifty out. That was enough altitude. He kept the nose down as he clawed for speed in the thin air at eleven thousand feet.

"Totally worth it," one of the D-boys announced as soon as he was on the Chinook's internal intercom.

He'd have to remember to tell that to the two Black Hawks flying guard for him…when they were in a friendly country and could risk a radio transmission. This deep inside China—or rather Chinese-held territory as the CIA's mission-briefing spook had insisted on calling it—radios attracted attention and were only used to avoid imminent death and destruction.

"Great, now I just need to get us out of this alive."

"Do that, Pete. We'd appreciate it."

He wished to hell he had a stealth bird like the one that had gone into bin Laden's compound. But the one that had crashed during that raid had been blown up. Where there was one, there were always two, but the second had gone back into hiding as thoroughly as if it had never existed. He hadn't heard a word about it since.

The Tibetan terrain was amazing, even if all he could see of it was the monochromatic green of night vision. And blackness. The largest city in Tibet lay a mere ten kilometers away and they were flying over barren wilderness. He could crash out here and no one would know for decades unless some yak herder stumbled upon them. Or were yaks in Mongolia? He was a corn-fed, white boy from Colorado, what did he know about Tibet? Most of the countries he'd flown into on black ops missions he'd only seen at night anyway.

While moving very, very fast.

Like now.

The inside of his visor was painted with overlapping readouts. A pre-defined terrain map, the best that modern satellite imaging could build made the first layer. This wasn't some crappy, on-line, look-at-a-picture-of-your-house display. Someone had a pile of dung outside their goat pen? He could see it, tell you how high it was, and probably say if they were pygmy goats or full-size LaManchas by the size of their shit-pellets if he zoomed in.

On top of that were projected the forward-looking infrared camera images. The FLIR imaging gave him a real-time overlay, in case someone had put an addition onto their goat shed since the last satellite pass, or parked their tractor across his intended flight path.

His nervous system was paying autonomic attention to that combined landscape. He also compensated for the thin air at altitude as he instinctively chose when to start his climb over said goat shed or his swerve around it.

It was the third layer, the tactical display that had most of his attention. At least he and the two Black Hawks flying escort on him were finally on the move.

To insert this deep into Tibet, without passing over Bhutan or Nepal, they'd had to add wingtanks on the Black Hawks' hardpoints where he'd much rather have a couple banks of

Hellfire missiles. Still, they had 20mm chain guns and the crew chiefs had miniguns which was some comfort.

While the action team was busy infiltrating the capital city and gathering intelligence on the particularly brutal Chinese assistant administrator, he and his crews had been squatting out in the wilderness under a camouflage net designed to make his helo look like just another god-forsaken Himalayan lump of granite.

Command had determined that it was better for the helos to wait on site through the day than risk flying out and back in. He and his crew had stood shifts on guard duty, but none of them had slept. They'd been flying together too long to have any new jokes, so they'd played a lot of cribbage. He'd long ago ruled no gambling on a mission, after a fistfight had broken out about a bluff hand that cost a Marine three hundred and forty-seven dollars. Marines hated losing to Army no matter how many times it happened. They'd had to sit on him for a long time before he calmed down.

Tonight's mission was part of an on-going campaign to discredit the Chinese "presence" in Tibet on the international stage—as if occupying the country the last sixty years didn't count toward ruling, whether invited or not. As usual, there was a crucial vote coming up at the U.N.—that, as usual, the Chinese could be guaranteed to ignore. However, the ever-hopeful CIA was in a hurry to make sure that any damaging information that they could validate was disseminated as thoroughly as possible prior to the vote.

Not his concern.

His concern was, were they going to pass over some Chinese sentry post at their top speed of a hundred and ninety-six miles an hour? The sentries would then call down a couple Shenyang J-16 jet fighters that could hustle along at Mach 2 to fry his sorry ass. He knew there was a pair of them parked at Lhasa along with some older gear that would be just as effective against his three helos.

"Don't suppose you could get a move on, Pete?"

"Eat shit, Nicolai!" He was a good man to have as a copilot. Pete knew he was holding on too tight, and Nicolai knew that a joke was the right way to ease the moment.

He, Nicolai, and the four pilots in the two Black Hawks had a long way to go tonight and he'd never make it if he stayed so tight on the controls that he could barely maneuver. Pete eased off and felt his fingers tingle with the rush of returning blood. They dove down into gorges and followed them as long as they dared. They hugged cliff walls at every opportunity to decrease their radar profile. And they climbed.

That was the true danger—they would be up near the helos' limits when they crossed over the backbone of the Himalayas in their rush for India. The air was so rarefied that they burned fuel at a prodigious rate. Their reserve didn't allow for any extended battles while crossing the border…not for any battle at all really.

# # #

It was pitch dark outside her helicopter when Captain Danielle Delacroix stamped on the left rudder pedal while giving the big Chinook right-directed control on the cyclic. It tipped her most of the way onto her side, but let her continue in a straight line. A Chinook's rotors were sixty feet across—front to back they overlapped to make the spread a hundred feet long. By cross-controlling her bird to tip it, she managed to execute a straight line between two mock pylons only thirty feet apart. They were made of thin cloth so they wouldn't down the helo if you sliced one—she was the only trainee to not have cut one yet.

At her current angle of attack, she took up less than a half-rotor of width, just twenty-four feet. That left her nearly three feet to either side, sufficient as she was moving at under a hundred knots.

The training instructor sitting beside her in the copilot's seat didn't react as she swooped through the training course at Fort Campbell, Kentucky. Only child of a single mother, she was used to providing her own feedback loops, so she didn't expect anything else. Those who expected outside validation rarely survived the SOAR induction testing, never mind the two years of training that followed.

As a loner kid, Danielle had learned that self-motivated congratulations and fun were much easier to come by than external ones. She'd spent innumerable hours deep in her mind as a pre-teen superheroine. At twenty-nine she was well on her way to becoming a real life one, though Helo-girl had never been a character she'd thought of in her youth.

External validation or not, after two years of training with the U.S. Army's 160th Special Operations Aviation Regiment she was ready for some action. At least *she* was convinced that she was. But the trainers of Fort Campbell, Kentucky had not signed off on anyone in her trainee class yet.

Nor had they given any hint of when they might.

She ducked ten tons of racing Chinook under a bridge and bounced into a near vertical climb to clear the power line on the far side. Like a ride on the toboggan at Terrassee Dufferin during *Le Carnaval de Québec*, only with five thousand horsepower at her finger-tips. Using her Army signing bonus—the first money in her life that was truly hers—to attend *Le Carnaval* had been her one trip back to her birthplace since her mother took them to America when she was ten.

To even apply to SOAR required five years of prior military rotorcraft experience. She had applied after seven years because of a chance encounter—or rather what she'd thought was a chance encounter at the time.

Captain Justin Roberts had been a top Chinook pilot, the one who had convinced her to switch from her beloved Black Hawk and try out the massive twin-rotor craft. One flight and she'd been a goner, begging her commander until he gave in and let her cross over to the new platform. Justin had made the jump from the 10th Mountain Division to the 160th SOAR not long after that.

Then one night she'd been having pizza in Watertown, New York a couple miles off the 10th's base at Fort Drum.

"Danielle?" Justin had greeted her with the surprise of finding a good friend in an unexpected place. Danielle had liked Justin—even if he was a too-tall, too-handsome cowboy and completely knew it. But "good friend" was unusual for Danielle, with anyone, and Justin came close.

"Captain Roberts," as a dry greeting over the top edge of her Suzanne Brockmann novel didn't faze him in the slightest.

"Mind if I join ya?" A question he then answered for himself by sliding into the opposite seat and taking a slice of her pizza. She been thinking of taking the leftovers back to base, but that was now an idle thought.

"Are you enjoying life in SOAR?" she did her best to appear a normal, social human, a skill she'd learned by rote. *Greeting someone you knew after a time apart? Ask a question about them.* "They treating you well?"

"Whoo-ee, you have no idea, Danielle," his voice was smooth as…well, always…so she wouldn't think about it also sounding like a pickup line. He was beautiful, but didn't interest her; the outgoing ones never did.

"Tell me." *Men love to talk about themselves, so let them.*

And he did. But she'd soon forgotten about her novel, and would have forgotten the pizza if he hadn't reminded her to eat.

His stories shifted from intriguing to fascinating. There was a world out there that she'd been only peripherally aware of. The Night Stalkers of the 160th SOAR weren't simply better helicopter pilots, they were the most highly-trained and best-equipped ones on the planet. Their missions were pure razor's edge and black-op dark.

He'd left her with a hundred questions and enough interest to fill out an application to the 160th. Being a decent guy, Justin even paid for the pizza after eating half.

The speed at which she was rushed into testing told her that her meeting with Justin hadn't been by chance and that she owed him more than half a pizza next time they met. She'd asked after him a couple of times since she'd made it past the qualification exams— and the examiners' brutal interviews that had left her questioning her sanity, never mind her ability.

"Justin Roberts is presently deployed, ma'am," was the only response she'd ever gotten.

Now that she was through training—almost, had to be soon, didn't it?—Danielle realized that was probably less of an evasion and more likely to do with the brutal op tempo the Night Stalkers maintained. The SOAR 1st Battalion had just won the coveted Lt. General Ellis D. Parker awards for Outstanding Combat Aviation Battalion *and* Aviation Battalion of the Year. They'd been on deployment every single day of the last year, actually of the last decade-plus since 9/11.

The very first Special Forces boots on the ground in Afghanistan were delivered that October by the Night Stalkers and nothing had slacked off since. Justin might be in the 5th battalion D company, but they were just as heavily assigned as the 1st.

Part of their training had included tours in Afghanistan. But unlike their prior deployments, these were brief, intense, and then they'd be back in the States pushing to integrate their new skills.

SOAR needed her training to end and so did she.

Danielle was ready for the job, in her own, inestimable opinion. But she wasn't going to get there until the trainers signed off that she'd reached fully mission-qualified proficiency.

The Fort Campbell training course was never set up the same from one flight to the next, but it always had a time limit. The time would be short and they didn't tell you what it was. So she drove the Chinook for all it was worth like Regina Jaquess waterskiing her way to U.S. Ski Team Female Athlete of the Year.

The Night Stalkers were a damned secretive lot, and after two years of training, she understood why. With seven years flying for the 10th, she'd thought she was good.

She'd been repeatedly lauded as one of the top pilots at Fort Drum.

The Night Stalkers had offered an education in what it really meant to fly. In the two years of training, she'd flown more hours than in the seven years prior, despite two deployments to Iraq. And spent more time in the classroom than her life-to-date accumulated flight hours.

But she was ready now. It was *très viscérale,* right down in her bones she could feel it. The Chinook was as much a part of her nervous system as breathing.

Too bad they didn't build men the way they built the big Chinooks—especially the MH-47G which were built specifically to SOAR's requirements. The aircraft were steady, trustworthy, and the most immensely powerful helicopters deployed in the U.S. Army—what more could a girl ask for? But finding a superhero man to go with her superhero helicopter was just a fantasy for a lonely teenage girl.

She dove down into a canyon and slid to a hover mere inches over the reservoir inside the thirty-second window laid out on the flight plan.

Danielle resisted a sigh. She was ready for something to happen and to happen soon.

# # #

Pete's Chinook and his two escort Black Hawks crossed into the mountainous province of Sikkim, India ten feet over the glaciers and still moving fast. It was an hour before dawn, they'd made it out of China while it was still dark.

"Twenty minutes of fuel remaining," Nicolai said it like a personal challenge when they hit the border.

"Thanks, I never would have noticed."

It had been a nail-biting tradeoff: the more fuel he burned, the more easily he climbed due to the lighter load. The more he climbed, the faster he burned what little fuel remained.

Safe in Indian airspace he climbed hard as Nicolai counted down the minutes remaining, burning fuel even faster than he had been while crossing the mountains of southern Tibet. They caught up with the U.S. Air Force

HC-130P Combat King refueling tanker with only ten minutes of fuel left.

"Ram that bitch," Nicolai called out.

Pete extended the refueling probe which reached only a few feet beyond the forward edge of the rotor blade and drove at the basket trailing behind the tanker on its long hose.

He nailed it on the first try despite the fluky winds. Striking the valve in the basket with over four hundred pounds of pressure, a clamp snapped over the refueling probe and Jet A fuel shot into his tanks.

His helo had the least fuel due to having the most men aboard, so he was first in line. His Number Two picked up the second refueling basket trailing off the other wing of the Combat King. Thirty seconds and three hundred gallons later and he was breathing much more easily.

"Ah," Nicolai sighed. "It is better than the sex," his thick Russian accent only ever surfaced in this moment or in a bar while picking up women.

"Hey, Nicolai," Nicky the Greek called over the intercom from his crew chief position seated behind Pete. "Do you make love in Russian?"

A question Pete had always been careful to avoid.

"For you, I make special exception." That got a laugh over the system.

Which explained why Pete always kept his mouth shut at this moment.

"The ladies, Nicolai? What about the ladies?" Alfie the portside gunner asked.

"Ah," he sighed happily as he signaled that the other choppers had finished their refueling and formed up to either side, "the ladies love the Russian. They don't need to know I grew up in Maryland and I learn my great-great-grandfather's native tongue at the University called Virginia."

He sounded so pleased that Pete wished he'd done the same rather than study Japanese and Mandarin.

Another two hours of—thank god—straight-and-level flight at altitude through the breaking dawn and they landed on the aircraft carrier awaiting them in the Bay of Bengal. India had agreed to turn a blind eye as long as the Americans never actually touched their soil.

Once standing on the deck—and the worst of the kinks had been worked out—he pulled his team together: six pilots and seven crew chiefs.

"Honor to serve!" He saluted them sharply.

"Hell yeah!" They shouted in response and saluted in turn. It was their version of spiking the football in the end zone.

A petty officer in a bright green vest appeared at his elbow, "Follow me please, sir." He pointed toward the Navy-gray command structure that towered above the carrier's deck. The Commodore of the entire carrier group was waiting for him just outside the entrance. Not a good idea to keep a One-Star waiting, so he waved at the team.

"See you in the mess for dinner," he shouted to the crew over the noise of an F-18 Hornet fighter jet trapping on the #2 wire. After two days of surviving on MREs while squatting on the Tibetan tundra, he was ready for a steak, a burger, a mountain of pasta, whatever. Or maybe all three.

The green escorted him across the hazards

of the busy flight deck. Pete had kept his helmet on to buffer the noise, but even at that he winced as another Hornet fired up and was flung aloft by the catapult.

"Orders, Major Napier," the Commodore handed him a folded sheet the moment he arrived. "Hate to lose you."

The Commodore saluted, which Pete automatically returned before looking down at the sheet of paper in his hands. The man was gone before the import of Pete's orders slammed in.

A different green-clad deckhand showed up with Pete's duffle bag and began guiding him toward a loading C-2 Greyhound twin-prop airplane. It was parked number two for the launch catapult, close behind the raised jet-blast deflector.

His crew, being led across in the opposite direction to return to the berthing decks below, looked at him aghast.

"Stateside," was all he managed to gasp out as they passed.

A stream of foul cursing followed him from behind. Their crew was tight. Why the hell was Command breaking it up?

And what in the name of fuck-all had he done to deserve this?

He glanced at the orders again as he stumbled up the Greyhound's rear ramp and crash landed into a seat.

Training rookies?

It was worse than a demotion.

This was punishment.

This and other titles are available at fine retailers everywhere.

Other works by M.L. Buchman

Delta Force
Target Engaged

Firehawks
Pure Heat
Wildfire at Dawn
Full Blaze
Wildfire at Larch Creek
Wildfire on the Skagit
Hot Point
Flash of Fire

The Night Stalkers
The Night Is Mine
I Own the Dawn
Daniel's Christmas
Wait Until Dark
Frank's Independence Day
Peter's Christmas
Take Over at Midnight
Light Up the Night
Bring On the Dusk
Target of the Heart
Target Lock on Love
Christmas at Peleliu Cove
Zachary's Christmas

By Break of Day

Angelo's Hearth
Where Dreams are Born
Where Dreams Reside
Maria's Christmas Table
Where Dreams Unfold
Where Dreams Are Written

Eagle Cove
Return to Eagle Cove
Recipe for Eagle Cove

Deities Anonymous
Cookbook from Hell: Reheated
Saviors 101

Thrillers
Swap Out!
One Chef!
Two Chef!

SF/F Titles
Nara
Monk's Maze

Newsletter signup at:
www.mlbuchman.com

www.ingramcontent.com/pod-product-compliance
Lightning Source LLC
Chambersburg PA
CBHW050501110726
47899CB00003B/1036